CW01494895

MATT MCAFEE

Murder At The Manor

First published by Independent 2021

Copyright © 2021 by Matt McAfee

All rights reserved. No part of this publication may be reproduced, stored or transmitted in any form or by any means, electronic, mechanical, photocopying, recording, scanning, or otherwise without written permission from the publisher. It is illegal to copy this book, post it to a website, or distribute it by any other means without permission.

This novel is entirely a work of fiction. The names, characters and incidents portrayed in it are the work of the author's imagination. Any resemblance to actual persons, living or dead, events or localities is entirely coincidental.

First edition

ISBN: 9798487033314

This book was professionally typeset on Reedsy.
Find out more at reedsy.com

Dedicated to the 2021 Cast and Crew of the Columbus Community High School Drama Club. This project would have been impossible without your inspiration.

Contents

I

ACT 1

1

SCENE 1

(Setting: MOORE narrating in front of curtain.)

MOORE: You are about to be an eyewitness to a crime. The eccentric billionaire, Richard Billingsley III, will not leave this day alive...but he does not know that yet. This day starts off strangely enough. Four unique individuals will receive an invitation for dinner at the legendary Billingsley estate. If only he had known that one of his guests might have been a murderer. The first invitation goes to Mr. Steven Wright, a struggling businessman and former colleague (emphasis on the former) of Mr. Billingsley. Next there is Madam Maria Rinaldi, a recently widowed aristocrat who is in dire financial straits. Then there is Lady Dimitri. Lady Dimitri is a professed psychic who has more failures than successes to her name. The last to receive his invitation is, well, me. Hi, I'm

Eric Moore, and you are listening to my true-crime podcast "There's Moore To The Story." Decades ago, Mr. Billingsley's wife disappeared mysteriously. There is talk around town that she was murdered. I'm here to get to the bottom of it. With this odd group of invited guests, certainly the night would be interesting. But no one, I imagine, would've thought it would end in murder. *(MOORE exits. Curtain opens.)*

(Setting: Billingsley Manor. Butler MATTHEW PENNYS-WORTH is tidying up for the dinner party. Doorbell rings. PENNYSWORTH answers.)

PENNYSWORTH: Welcome Mr. Steven Wright! Mr. Wright, I am so glad that you made time in your schedule to join Mr. Billingsley for dinner tonight.

WRIGHT: *(Annoyed and aggravated)* It's the least he could do, that son of a gun. After years of business partnership, he....he....UGH...where's the booze?

PENNYSWORTH: Horderves and refreshments are on the table. Please make yourself at home.

WRIGHT: *(Grumbles and storms to the table where he shovels horderves into his mouth, and drinks as much champagne as he can stomach. He notices nice silverware on the table, and proceeds to put them into*

4

his pocket. Doorbell rings. PENNYSWORTH answers.)

PENNYSWORTH: Welcome Mrs. Maria Rinaldi!

RINALDI: That is MISS Rinaldi, young man. Mr. Rinaldi passed away late last year.

PENNYSWORTH: My sincerest apologies, MISS Rinaldi.

RINALDI: All is forgiven...um...what did you say your name was?

PENNYSWORTH: Pennysworth. Matthew Pennysworth. I am Mr. Billingsley's butler.

RINALDI: Oh wonderful. Marcus, please be a dear and take this. *(Thrusts her coat to him)*

PENNYSWORTH: It's Ma...yes ma'am. *(Leaves taking coat. RINALDI introduces herself to WRIGHT who is still shoveling food and drink into his mouth).*

RINALDI: *(Flirty)* My goodness, will you save some for lil ol' me?

WRIGHT: *(Grunts, continues eating)*

5

RINALDI: *(Still flirty. Extends hand.)* My name is Miss Maria Rinaldi, and who might you be.

WRIGHT: *(Extends hand)* Steven Wright.

RINALDI: Now where did you learn your matters? Did your mother never teach you that you never greet a lady sitting down.

WRIGHT: *(Annoyed because she is right, stands up)* Excuse me, Madam. It is nice to meet you *(kisses her hand)*.

RINALDI: *(Flirty)* I knew it. I knew there must be a gentleman in there somewhere. *(WRIGHT pulls out chair next to him for RINALDI. Doorbell rings. Matthew hurries to answer)*.

PENNYSWORTH: Welcome Lady Dimitri!

DIMITRI: *(Head in the clouds, trying to receive a revelation from the spirits)* Oooooh. What are you saying? Speak to me. Tell me the secrets from the other side. *(Snaps out of the trance)* What is your name, young man?

PENNYSWORTH: Matthew Pennysworth, ma'am.

DIMITRI: *(Excitedly)* Yes! I knew that. The spirits are telling me a letter. It's the letter.....B. B! Does your mother's name start with a B?

PENNYSWORTH: No.

DIMITRI: Of course not! I meant Father?

PENNYSWORTH: No.

DIMITRI: Siblings? *(PENNYSWORTH shakes his head.)* Aunts? *(PENNYSWORTH shakes his head.)* Uncles? *(PENNYSWORTH shakes his head.)* Grandparents? *(PENNYSWORTH shakes his head.)* Best friends? *(PEN-NYSWORTH shakes his head.)*

PENNYSWORTH: *(Embarrassed for DIMITRI)* Oh! I had a dog named Buddy.

DIMITRI: That's it! I knew it.

PENNYSWORTH: That was certainly impressive. Please let me take your coat, and make yourself at home. *(Doorbell rings. PENNYSWORTH answers.)* Welcome, Mr. Eric Moore! Mr. Moore, thank you for making time in your schedule to be our guest tonight.

MOORE: To be honest, I was shocked. I have been trying to get an interview with Mr. Billingsley for months, and he has evaded all attempts to contact him.

PENNYSWORTH: Mr. Billingsley is a very important and busy man, but you're persistence certainly has made an impression on him.

MOORE: *(Pulling out voice recorder)* Would you like to be interviewed? What have you heard about the rumors of a murder taking place on these grounds fifty years ago?

PENNYSWORTH: *(Oven dings).* I am so sorry. Dinner is ready and must be taken out of the oven. Please have a seat and make yourself at home.

MOORE: *(Embarrassingly approaches RINALDI and WRIGHT who are shamelessly flirting, and reaches for an horderve).* I am sorry to interrupt, but these look delicious.

WRIGHT: *(Noticeably in a better mood)* You're not interrupting anything. I am Mr. Steven Wright, and this lovely lady is my new friend...

RINALDI: *(Wanting to introduce herself)* I am Miss

8

Maria Rinaldi.

MOORE: *(Shakes their hands)* Pleasure to meet you both. Rinaldi. Are you, by chance, related to Gregory Rinaldi, the actor?

RINALDI: *(Nods yes)* Yes. He was my husband.

MOORE: I am so sorry for your loss.

RINALDI: Thank you. You know it was my husband's last wish *(looks flirtingly at WRIGHT)* for me to move on and be happy.

MOORE: Mr. Wright, how do you know Mr. Billingsley?

WRIGHT: Remember, the company B&W Incorporated?

MOORE: That sounds familiar.

WRIGHT: The B&W stood for Billingsley and Wright. I am Wright.

MOORE: I thought the company was simply called Billingsley Enterprises.

WRIGHT: *(Aggravated)* It is now. About twos decades ago, he kicked me out of a business that I helped found. *(Punches table)*

RINALDI: *(Concerned)* Oh, Steven. That's awful. But thankfully, you had your millions to comfort you?

WRIGHT: Are you kidding? All of my wealth was in B&W stock. When they kicked me out, I lost my stock options. I am flat broke!

RINALDI: *(Suddenly loses interest)* Oh, that's awful. Well, it was very nice to meet you. *(Goes to mirror and freshens up.)*

MOORE: *(Turns around and is scared by DIMITRI who is standing right behind him, faking a trance)* Ahh!

DIMITRI: I see...I see...I see....

MOORE: *(To WRIGHT)* What is happening?

WRIGHT: Who knows?

DIMITRI: I see...*(snaps out of trance)* You *(pointing at Eric)*. I saw you driving here in a blue Prius, am I correct?

10

MOORE: No.

DIMITRI: Oh...did you perhaps drive past a blue Prius on the way here?

MOORE: I mean, possibly?

DIMITRI: Yes, I see it clearly now. You drove past a blue Prius on the way here. Thank you, other world for your revelation!

PENNYSWORTH: *(carrying turkey)* Please everyone, have a seat. Dinner is being served. *(Guests sit down around the table, chit chatting to themselves)* Mr. Billingsley will be down in a moment. I understand that you all may be confused as to why you are here.

ALL GUESTS: Murmur. Why? What am I doing here? Etc.

PENNYSWORTH: All of those questions will be answered shortly. Mr. Billingsley is finishing up his evening routine, and will be down here shortly to greet you. *(Leaves for Kitchen)*

MOORE: Why are we all here tonight?

WRIGHT: Who knows. I haven't talked to Billingsley

11

in years. This is all so strange.

DIMITRI: Neither have I, not since he tried to ruin my reputation.

MOORE: What?

DIMITRI: Years ago, Billingsley came to visit my office for some guidance in his business deals. The spirits told me clearly to invest into a company. Letter by letter, the spelled it out. Invest in...E...N...R....O....N....ENRON.

WRIGHT: Oh jees. *(Head in hands)*

DIMITRI: The day after he purchased the stocks, the company crumbled to the ground, and Mr. Billingsley lost millions. The next day, he got on national television and ran my name and my business into the ground.

WRIGHT: Wait, wait, wait...I know you...you're not Lady Dimitri...You are Madam McAdams...you're the idiot psychic! *(begins to laugh uncontrollably)*

DIMITRI: *(Angry)* I am not! *(To Moore)* You see what he did...he forever tainted my name, and ruined my business. I had to change my name, and I'm still struggling to be where I once was. I am not sure why we are invited here, but it better be good.

PENNYSWORTH: Welcome, your host for the evening, Mr. Richard Billingsley. *(All guest stand as he enters)*

BILLINGSLEY: Thank you all for coming. I hope that you have enjoyed eating my food, and perhaps laughing at my expense. *(Complete silence)* I suppose I deserve that. Please have a seat. *(All guests sit down)* I'm sure you all are wondering why I brought you here today. I want to say up front that it isn't easy to invite you all here. Some of you are very angry with me and some are suspicious of me. It's not easy for me to look into your faces knowing what I have done.

One month ago, my doctor gave me one year to live. I have an incurable disease that is making its way through my body. Since that time, I have reflected deeply on my life. I have so much that every man wants. Money, status, fame. But that came through years of deceit, and treating others poorly. In the few remaining months of my life, I want to live with a clean conscience. I want to make things right.

Steven. Everything I have, I have because of you. For years, you and I worked together, hand in hand, and we built an empire together. But I was poisoned by greed, and I wanted the whole pie for myself, so I cut you out and left you with nothing. I have rewritten my will, and am leaving half of what I have to you. It is the half you deserved anyway.

Maria. We have known each other for a long time. I was a widower in love with a married woman, who also happened to be one of my best friends. When Gregory died, I didn't reach out, not because I didn't want to, but because I wanted to respect my friend and honor his widow. But I am so glad that you are here now, and before I died, I needed to tell you how I feel.

Madam McAdams, after the Enron debacle, I made it my life's mission to single-handedly ruin your reputation. Every chance I received on every platform available to me, I dragged your name through the mud. There is no excuse for all the things I said to you and about you. Tomorrow morning, I am calling together a press conference, and publicly apologizing for the way I have treated you.

Eric, you have called my office every day, multiple times a day for months, asking about the disappearance of my wife. I understand that with her disappearance came rumors and accusations towards me. I'm sure you can understand why I didn't want to relive the pain of my past. After dinner tonight, I have made time where we can sit down, and you can ask any question you want. I want to put this all behind me.

In any way I can, I want to make it right, so will you please forgive an old dying man, like me? *(All guests are silent)*

WRIGHT: *(Stands up and breaks the silence)* Richard, for years, I have held onto bitterness and anger towards you for what you did for me. I prayed that one day I would be able to look you into your eyes and tell you what I really thought about you. Now, I'm here, and when I look into your eyes, I know longer see the man I once knew. I forgive you.

DIMITRI: *(Ethereal. Head in the clouds)* Yes, yes, yes! I hear the spirits. They are speaking to me...C....H....A...N...G..E..D. Changed. The spirits say you have changed. I too forgive you. They also say not to worry! For your change of heart will result in good fortune!

BILLINGSLEY: *(Starts to laugh. Louder and louder and more maniacal. People unsure begin to laugh with him.)*

MOORE: *(To Rinaldi)* Why are we laughing?

RINALDI: I haven't the faintest idea.

BILLINGSLEY: You fools. You fools! I knew you were all suckers, but I didn't think you were this weak.

WRIGHT: What is going on?

BILLINGSLEY: Did you really think I brought you all here to apologize? *(Laughter)* I brought you all here so I can rub it in your faces that I won. I won. Steven, you're never getting your half. I'm spending every last penny to enjoy my final days in luxury. And when you one day die as a poor man, I want you to remember that I won! McAdams, you still are the worst psychic I've ever seen. You couldn't forecast yesterday's weather! Eric, you can kiss my old behind. And Maria, don't think I don't know you're here to get after my money. Pennysworth!

PENNYSWORTH: Yes, Mr. Billingsley.

BILLINGSLEY: Please escort my "guests" out of my house.

PENNYSWORTH: But Mr. Billingsley, it has become quite stormy outside.

BILLINGSLEY: Did I stutter? Do as I say now. Good-bye losers. Great knowing you! *(Thunder roars. Lights go out. Pennysworth screams. Billingsley screams. Lights come back on. Billingsley is dead, slumped over with his face in his food, with knife wounds in his back. Matthew Pennysworth is passed out on the floor with* *knife wounds as well. Everyone screams.)*

2

SCENE 2

MOORE: Whoa, whoa, whoa, whoa.

RINALDI: Oh my stars, Richard. *(Checks pulse)* He's, he's dead!

WRIGHT: What about the butler? *(Checks vitals)* He's unconscious, and his heart rate is low.

MOORE: It appears that both Mr. Billingsley and Pennysworth are suffering from knife wounds. I'll call the police.

DIMITRI: Oh, yes, yes, I see it now....

RINALDI: What?

DIMITRI: I see...yes...oh poor Matthew....he was

caught in between the attacker and Mr. Billingsley.

RINALDI: Do you see the attackers face?

DIMITRI: *(Trying to focus)* It's...very...fuzzy....

WRIGHT: Of course it is, Madam Enron.

RINALDI: Ya know, I don't need a spirit to tell me who killed Mr. Billingsley and my financial future!

WRIGHT: What are you implying?

RINALDI: You admitted you were angry with Richard for the way he treated you.

DIMITRI: That is your motive...for murder!

WRIGHT: Oh give me a break. I don't have any more motive than any other person.

DIMITRI: The spirits...the spirits...the spirits say.....

WRIGHT: The spirits aren't talking to you, you crazy old bag.

DIMITRI: My heavens!

RINALDI: Don't speak to her that way!

WRIGHT: Did we not forget how she just prophesied that Billingsley was going to have good fortune in his future? She's not a psychic, she's just off her meds.

MOORE: *(Hangs up phone)* I've got good news and bad news.

RINALDI: I don't think I can handle any more bad news.

MOORE: The good news is the police and ambulance are on their way.

DIMITRI: And the bad news?

WRIGHT: Shouldn't you already know?

DIMITRI: Why I never....

WRIGHT: What's the bad news?

MOORE: The storm has knocked over a tree that is blocking the only road leading to the manor.

WRIGHT: Great. The only thing worse than having dinner with Billingsley, is being stuck with his annoying guests.

RINALDI: Perhaps, you should have thought of that before you killed him.

WRIGHT: I didn't kill him! I had no more motive than anyone else in this room. He embarrassed and humiliated all of us tonight. It could have been any of us.

RINALDI: Lady Dimitri, perhaps you can reach Richard on the other side. Perhaps he can tell us who killed him.

DIMITRI: I can certainly try. *(Trance)* Oh, I see him. I see Mr. Billingsley. He's saying something....It....Is... Hot...Down...Here....It is hot down here!

WRIGHT: Ha! Now that I can believe.

MOORE: Ok, let's knock it off, and be serious. We first need to stabilize Pennysworth. Steven, you and I get him to the couch. Maria, Lady Dimitri find a first aid kit, and some water. *(WRIGHT and MOORE move PENNYSWORTH to a couch. RINALDI and DIMITRI come in with first aid kit.)*

RINALDI: Move aside. Many years ago, before I met

Gregory, I worked as a CNA. I can handle patching him up.

DIMITRI: No, no, no!

MOORE: What's the problem?

DIMITRI: I see...I see...he's on his way to the other side. Stay with us Matthew! *(Throws cup of water in his face)*

PENNYSWORTH: *(Gasps)*

EVERYONE: He's awake!

PENNYSWORTH: *(Weakly)* What happened? What's going on?

MOORE: Someone tried to attack Mr. Billingsley, and you were caught in the middle.

RINALDI: Did you see who did it?

WRIGHT: Tell them it wasn't me!

PENNYSWORTH: *(Shakes his head and falls back asleep)*

MOORE: He needs to get rest. Maria, do you think he'll be ok until the ambulance arrives?

MARIA: The bleeding has stopped, and his heart rate is more regular. We've bought him some time.

MOORE: Ok, everyone around this table right now. *(Everyone circles up around this table. Moore lays out voice recorder)* Ok. One of us is a murderer. Murderer say what? (Silence). Dang, I was kind of hoping that would work. Ok. Mr. Billingsley and Pennysworth were stabbed. The murder weapon is missing. Let's empty our pockets onto the table. I'll start. I have a wallet, keys, extra SD card for my voice recorder, and a moist towelette in case we had chicken wings tonight. Maria?

RINALDI: *(Empties purse)* Wallet, keys, jewelry, lipstick, perfume, and um a book.

MOORE: Lay it out please. *(Rinaldi lays out book on table)*

WRIGHT: 101 Ways to Attract a Wealthy Man? Are you serious?

RINADLI: Don't you judge me!

DIMITRI: Oh oh my turn! *(Empties sleeves)* Cards. Potions. *(Pulls a bunny out of her turban)* Mr. Fluffytail.

MOORE: That was oddly impressive. You're last to go, Steven.

WRIGHT: *(Grumbles)* Wallet. Keys. *(Reaches in pocket. Face goes white)*. And that's...that's it.

RINALDI: What are you hiding?

WRIGHT: Nothing!

DIMITRI: The spirits are telling me your pants are on fire.

MOORE: Come on, Steven.

WRIGHT: *(Pulls out a fork, a spoon, and a knife)*

RINALDI: *(Gasps)* I knew it!

WRIGHT: It was nice silverware! I wanted to steal from the guy. Not kill him.

DIMITRI: A likely story!

MOORE: Let me take a look at that knife. *(Grabs it*

with napkin) This knife is clean. And the blade is much too small to be the one that killed Billingsley.

WRIGHT: I told you!

MOORE: Well, we're back to square one. One of us is the murderer.

DIMITRI: What if we weren't?

MOORE: What are you talking about?

DIMITRI: Are you telling me you have never heard?

WRIGHT: Oh give me a break.

RINALDI: I heard, but I never thought it was possible.

MOORE: What are we talking about?

DIMITRI: *(Lights dim. Spotlight on Dimitri)* Evelyn.

THE REST: Evelyn?

DIMITRI: Evelyn! Years ago, before the riches, and before the billions, Richard was married to a sweet young lady named Evelyn.

MOORE: Yes, and she disappeared mysteriously.

DIMITRI: Disappeared? You poor naive fool! She didn't just disappear. She's dead.

RINALDI: Oh my!

DIMITRI: Oh my is right. There were rumors that Mr. Billingsley had done away with his wife because she no longer pleased him. But the spirits are telling me exactly what happened. Yes...yes..yes...I can see him. Everyday, putting a little poison in her morning tea. Everyday, she becomes sicker and sicker. She goes to doctors, but they cannot figure out what is wrong. Until one day, she goes to sleep, and never wakes up. She is buried somewhere on these grounds, and her spirit haunts these halls. I hear her calling from the other side now.... She is saying....R...E...V...E...N...G... E....REVENGE. Her spirit has crossed over to exact her revenge so she can finally rest at peace.

MOORE: What a fantastic story.

RINALDI: Could it be true?

WRIGHT: Great psychic detective work there, Madam.

DIMITRI: Why, thank you.

WRIGHT: There's only one problem.

DIMITRI: What's that?

WRIGHT: Evelyn isn't dead.

DIMITRI: Excuse me?

MOORE: What did you say?

WRIGHT: Evelyn isn't dead! She's living happily with her new husband in Hawaii. She's got kids, and grandkids. She's living her best life!

DIMITRI: But I heard...

WRIGHT: Yeah, you hear a lot of things, but I've been around for a while. Richard and I were still in business together when she "disappeared". She didn't die. She left him. He was a bully of a husband, and worked around the clock. She met a man at church and fell in love with him, and they've been together ever since. I still get Christmas cards from her.

RINALDI: Does her husband have a brother perchance?

MOORE: Oh, jees.

WRIGHT: So, while your theory makes a great plot for a horror movie. It's just not possible. *(Knock at the door startles everyone. In comes DET. SEBASTIAN WOLFE)*

WOLFE: Police! Hands up so I can see them! *(Everyone's hands are up)* I am Det. Sebastian Wolfe. I understand that there has been a murder.

MOORE: Yes sir. The deceased is right here, and there is another critically injured over there.

WOLFE: *(Radios in)* Send in the ambulance crew. *(Ambulance crew comes in and tends to PENNYSWORTH who is starting to wake up)* Ok, everyone put your hands behind their back. You all are coming to the station with me.

WRIGHT: Detective, there's been a misunderstanding.

DIMITRI: Yes, there is confusion in the spirit world.

RINALDI: Now, you wouldn't lock up little ol' me,

now would you?

WOLFE: *(As he is handcuffing people)* Everyone I would encourage you all to exercise a very important right at this moment?

MOORE: What's that?

WOLFE: The right to remain silent! *(Lights off. Curtain closes)*

3

SCENE 3

(*Setting: Police interrogation room. WRIGHT, RINALDI, MOORE, and DIMITRI are all sitting next to each other on one side of table*)

WRIGHT: I don't think I can take much more of this. We have been locked in here for hours.

RINALDI: Well, maybe if you hadn't killed him we wouldn't be in this mess.

WRIGHT: I didn't kill him, you gold-digging....

DIMITRI: Yes...yes...yes...I see it!

RINALDI: What do you see?

DIMITRI: I see a hero. One who will rescue us from

this room and set us free. He's coming down the hallway now. He will walk in through that door in 3... .2...1... *(Nothing happens)*

MOORE: *(Slams head on table)*

DIMITRI: 3...2...1... *(Nothing happens)*. I mean 3...2... *(Wolfe enters. Everyone jumps)*

WOLFE: Alright, alright. You've been in here long enough, I hope you've got your story straight. What exactly happened here tonight.

EVERYONE: *(Talks at the same time to give their side of the story.)*

WOLFE: Hey, hey, hey! Everyone settle down. Let me try this another way. You all were invited to Mr. Billingsley's house for dinner tonight, correct?

EVERYONE: Yes.

WOLFE: Great. Does anyone have their invitation on them?

DIMITRI: Oh, I do! *(Pulls out of sleeve. Endless handkerchiefs come instead)*. It's in here somewhere. *(Finally gets the invitation)*

WOLFE: Thank you. "Dear treasured guest, you are cordially invited to a banquet in your honor at the Billingsley Manor. Mr. Richard Billingsley III has personally requested your presence. Please arrive by 6:55pm. Your friend, Mr. Billingsley."

MOORE: That's odd.

WOLFE: What's odd?

MOORE: If the invitation was written personally by Mr. Billingsley, why does it refer to himself in the third person?

WRIGHT: Mr. Billingsley didn't write the invitations.

MOORE: No?

WRIGHT: Of course not. He probably had Pennysworth write them out.

MOORE: And even sign his name?

WRIGHT: Most likely.

MOORE: Mr. Billingsley said he recently rewrote his will. Has anyone seen it?

RINALDI: Did he actually rewrite it, or did he just say that to mess with us?

WOLFE: I'll call Mr. Billingsley's attorney to find out. One moment (leaves to make a phone call).

MOORE: Track with me. Mr. Billingsley has no family, no children, no friends. To whom does he leave his vast fortune? How about the servant that serves him hand and foot day after day, year after year.

WRIGHT: If that's the case then...

DIMITRI: It was Pennysworth! Pennysworth! I can see it clearly know! He wasn't in the way of the attacker. He is the attacker!

MOORE: We got to tell Detective Wolfe.

EVERYONE: *(Shouting for WOLFE)*

WOLFE: Hey! Hold your horses. Billingsley's attorney says his will was updated, and that the sole heir of his fortune is *(looks at notes)* one Matthew Pennysworth.

MOORE: Detective! Pennysworth....

DIMITRI: ...Is the attacker! The spirits told me!

RINALDI: Where is he now?

WOLFE: He was just released from the hospital. His injuries were merely flesh wounds.

MOORE: We need to get back to Billingsley Manor right away.

WOLFE: Hurry. Everyone come with me. *(Lights go out)*

4

SCENE 4

(SETTING: Billingsley Manor. PENNYSWORTH is packing up his things trying to get out of town. WOLFE and crew barges in)

WOLFE: Police. Show me your hands!

PENNYSWORTH: (Continues packing) About time you showed up. I almost thought this escape would have been too easy.

MOORE: We know it was you, Pennysworth. Give it up.

PENNYSWORTH: Yeah? How did you figure that out? The psychic tell you?

DIMITRI: (Proudly) I helped!

PENNYSWORTH: I doubt it.

MOORE: We know that you rewrote Mr. Billingsley's will to leave everything to you. Over the years sending out his letters, you had done a good job of mastering his signature. Virtually undetectable to the untrained eye.

PENNYSWORTH: You're smarter than you look, Eric. I deserve that money. Day after day, putting up with his incessant demands. I deserve it.

RINALDI: Why the dinner? Why invite us?

PENNYSWORTH: I needed patsies. I needed fall guys. I needed to keep the police off my trail until I got away. It seems like I'll need to resort to plan B *(pulls weapon)*. If you will excuse me, I need to make it to my flight. I have a long life to live, and a lot of money to do it.

DIMITRI: The spirits...the spirits...

PENNYSWORTH: Will you shut up! You are single-handedly the worst psychic I have ever seen.

DIMITRI: I hear the spirits...they are saying...3...2....

WRIGHT: *(comes behind PENNYSWORTH. PENNYS-WORTH turns around surprised)* ONE! *(Punches Pennysworth in the face. WOLFE tackles PENNYSWORTH and handcuffs him)*

WOLFE: You have the right to remain silent, anything you say can and will be used against you *(escorts PENNYSWORTH out)*

PENNYSWORTH: I'll get you for this! I'll get you all for this!

RINALDI: Oh my stars. *(goes to WRIGHT)* Why, Mr. Wright. I never knew you could be so strong. Why don't we leave here and get drinks? On me?

WRIGHT: That sounds wonderful. *(As they leave, they pass by DIMITRI)*. Madam McAdams, thank you for distracting him while I came in through the service entrance.

DIMITRI: The spirits told me you were coming! I saw you in a vision!

WRIGHT: Right. I'm sure you did. Well, thank you. Why don't you come with us and celebrate? Is that alright, Maria?

RINALDI: *(Slightly annoyed)* For tonight, but I do expect a proper date with you sometime soon.

WRIGHT: Of course. How about you Eric? You coming?

MOORE: You all go on ahead. I'll be there in a moment. *(Takes out voice recorder)* Mr. Billingsley was murdered today. I was there when it happened. He was a man of riches and status, but he lacked the things that truly make someone great. He lacked friends and a pure heart. He was killed by the person closest to him. How will you live your life? Will you live it simply for your own self-interest, or will you live it for the benefit of others around you? What is success really? Is it all the money in the world, or is it having the love and respect of those closest to you? And if that's truly what success is, how will that change your life? We'll ask that question and more, next time on "There's Moore To the Story". *(Curtains close. Blackout)*

END

CHARACTER LIST

MR. RICHARD BILLINGSLEY III

Billingsley is an aged and mean Billionaire with his fair share of enemies. Should be dressed sharply, yet comfortably.

MR. MATTHEW PENNYSWORTH

Pennysworth is Billingsley's loyal butler. Should be dressed in professional butler attire. This part can easily be adapted for a female.

MR. STEVEN WRIGHT

Wright is Billingsley's disgruntled, former business parter. Should be dressed in business casual clothing.

MS. MARIA RINALDI

Rinaldi is a widowed aristocrat trying to seduce Billingsley to secure her financial future. Should be dressed elegantly in formal wear.

LADY DIMITRI

Dimitri is a professed psychic who has a previous professional relationship with Billingsley. Should be dressed in gaudy attire as she always seeks to be center of attention.

MR. ERIC MOORE

Moore is a true-crime podcaster. Moore can be dressed casual, but stylish. This part can easily be adapted for a female.

DET. SEBASTIAN WOLFE

Wolfe is a homicide detective. Wolfe can be dressed business casual with clearly seen badge.

Printed in Great Britain
by Amazon

10437585R00027